THE BABY-SITTERS CLUB®

JESSI'S SECRET LANGUAGE

DON'T MISS THE OTHER BABY-SITTERS CLUB GRAPHIC NOVELS!

KRISTY'S GREAT IDEA

THE TRUTH ABOUT STACEY

MARY ANNE SAVES THE DAY

CLAUDIA AND MEAN JANINE

DAWN AND THE IMPOSSIBLE THREE

KRISTY'S BIG DAY

BOY-CRAZY STACEY

LOGAN LIKES MARY ANNE!

CLAUDIA AND THE NEW GIRL

KRISTY AND THE SNOBS

GOOD-BYE STACEY, GOOD-BYE

ANN M. MARTIN

THE BABY-SITTERS CLUB®

JESSI'S SECRET LANGUAGE

A GRAPHIC NOVEL BY

CHAN CHAU

WITH COLOR BY BRADEN LAMB AND SAM BENNETT

The font used in this graphic novel does not distinguish between upper- and lowercase letters. Please note that the word "Deaf," when referring to a person, is intended to have a capital D. This indicates someone who belongs to a community of people who share a common culture and use sign language as their primary method of communication.

The creators would like to thank Lynne Kelly for lending her expertise during the making of this book.

Library of Congress Control Number: 2021948452

ISBN 978-1-338-61608-8 (hardcover)
ISBN 978-1-338-61607-1 (paperback)

10 9 8 7 6 5 4 3 2 1   22 23 24 25 26

Printed in China 62
First edition, September 2022

Edited by Cassandra Pelham Fulton and David Levithan
Book design by Phil Falco
Publisher: David Saylor

For Cary

A. M. M.

For Danya, Alice, Maddi, Harry, Ben,
Brando, and Thomas. And to the lovely Erik,
who helped carry me through the making of this book.

C. C.

KRISTY THOMAS
PRESIDENT

CLAUDIA KISHI
VICE PRESIDENT

MARY ANNE SPIER
SECRETARY

DAWN SCHAFER
TREASURER

JESSI RAMSEY
JUNIOR OFFICER

MALLORY PIKE
JUNIOR OFFICER

CHAPTER 1
HI, I'M JESSICA DAVIS RAMSEY, BUT YOU CAN CALL ME JESSI.
WE USED TO LIVE IN OAKLEY, NEW JERSEY. THEN DADDY GOT A PROMOTION AT WORK, WHICH WAS GREAT, OF COURSE...
BUT IT MEANT MOVING HIM TO THE STAMFORD, CONNECTICUT, BRANCH OF THE COMPANY.
5:29
THAT'S HOW WE ENDED UP HERE IN STONEYBROOK.

THE NEW HOUSE IS BIGGER THAN THE ONE WE HAD IN OAKLEY, SO MY PARENTS SET UP THIS AREA IN THE BASEMENT SO THAT I CAN PRACTICE MY BALLET.

I LOVE SPENDING TIME DOWN HERE --

JUST THE BARRE AND ME.

FOR A WHILE, THINGS WERE A LITTLE ROUGH. IT WAS HARD TRYING TO MAKE NEW FRIENDS.
THEN I MET MALLORY PIKE. SHE'S MY NEW BEST FRIEND.
SHE INTRODUCED ME TO THE BABY-SITTERS CLUB, AND NOW WE'RE BOTH JUNIOR OFFICERS.

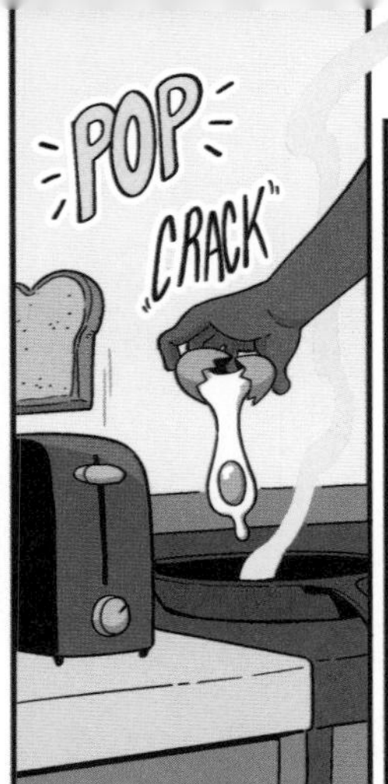
POP
"CRACK"

SIZZLE
CRACK
POP!

MORNING, SQUIRT.
OOH-BLAH.

LET'S GO SEE IF BECCA IS UP.

GO-BLOO?
COME ON, BREAKFAST IS ALMOST READY.
JESSI!

SO, TRYOUTS FOR THE BIG SHOW AT YOUR NEW DANCE SCHOOL TODAY?
YUP.

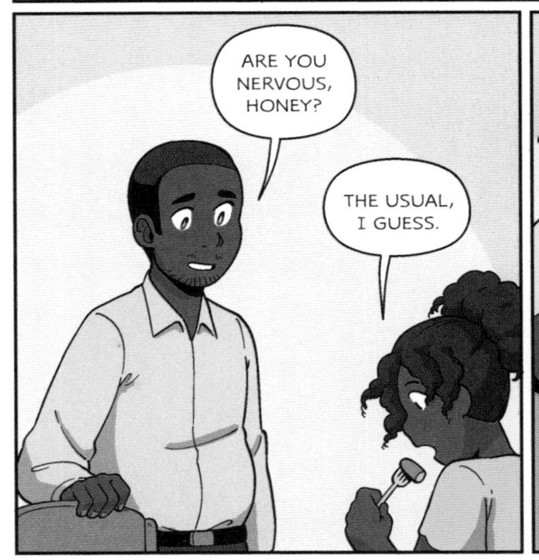
ARE YOU NERVOUS, HONEY?
THE USUAL, I GUESS.

UH-HUH...

WELL...MORE THAN THE USUAL.
IT'S NOT JUST THAT I WANT TO BE IN *COPPÉLIA*. IT'S ALSO THAT I DON'T KNOW HOW TRYOUTS ARE GOING TO GO.
THE BALLET SCHOOL THAT I CHOSE IN STAMFORD IS BIGGER AND MUCH MORE PROFESSIONAL AND COMPETITIVE THAN THE ONE IN OAKLEY.

WHAT'S *COPPÉLIA?*
OH, IT'S A GREAT BALLET. YOU'LL LOVE IT. WE'LL HAVE TO GO SEE IT, EVEN IF I DON'T MAKE THE CUT.

IT'S A STORY ABOUT A DOLLMAKER NAMED DR. COPPELIUS, THIS REALLY LIFELIKE DOLL HE CREATES -- THAT'S COPPÉLIA -- AND FRANZ, A HANDSOME YOUNG GUY WHO FALLS IN LOVE WITH THE DOLL. HE SEES HER FROM FAR AWAY AND THINKS SHE'S REAL.

THAT'S NOT THE ONLY PROBLEM, THOUGH. FRANZ IS ENGAGED TO SWANILDA, AND WHEN SHE THINKS FRANZ HAS FALLEN IN LOVE WITH ANOTHER WOMAN, SHE FEELS JEALOUS AND HURT.

THE STORY GETS SORT OF COMPLICATED AFTER THAT. IN THE END, EVERYTHING IS STRAIGHTENED OUT, AND SWANILDA AND FRANZ GET MARRIED, JUST LIKE THEY'D PLANNED.

AND LIVE HAPPILY EVER AFTER.

I JUST HOPE
I DON'T FALL OVER
MADAME NOELLE OR
CRASH INTO A MIRROR
OR SOMETHING.

I KNOW
YOU'LL DO FINE THIS
AFTERNOON, BABY.

OKAY, GIRLS.
TIME TO GET
A MOVE ON.

WHAT IS IT, BECCA?
MAMA, WE'RE HAVING A SPELLING BEE TODAY.
YOU'RE PROBABLY THE BEST SPELLER IN YOUR CLASS. DON'T WORRY.
BUT I CAN'T GET UP THERE IN FRONT OF EVERYONE.
THINK OF ME. I HAVE TO DANCE IN FRONT OF MY **WHOLE SCHOOL** TODAY.
DON'T FORGET -- I HAVE A BABY-SITTERS CLUB MEETING AFTER BALLET!

CHAPTER 2

HUFF
HUFF
HUFF
HUFF
I USUALLY RUSHED TO BSC MEETINGS FROM EITHER A BALLET CLASS OR A SITTING JOB.
DING-DONG
TAP
TAP
TAP
THANKS, JANINE.

HI! SORRY I'M LATE!
THAT'S OKAY. HAVE A SEAT.

EVEN THOUGH I HAD A REALLY BUSY SCHEDULE, JOINING THE CLUB WAS ONE OF THE BEST THINGS TO COME OUT OF MOVING TO STONEYBROOK.
CLAUDIA KISHI IS THE VICE PRESIDENT. SHE HAS A PRIVATE PHONE LINE AND HIDES LOTS OF CANDY IN HER ROOM.
DAWN SCHAFER BECAME THE TREASURER WHEN OUR FRIEND STACEY MCGILL MOVED BACK TO NEW YORK. DAWN IS A TRUE CALIFORNIA GIRL.
THIS IS MALLORY, WHO I MENTIONED BEFORE. SHE LOVES TO READ AND WRITE STORIES, AND HAS SEVEN SIBLINGS.

MARY ANNE SPIER IS THE SECRETARY. SHE'S IN CHARGE OF KEEPING THE CLUB NOTEBOOK IN ORDER. HER BOYFRIEND, LOGAN BRUNO, IS AN ASSOCIATE MEMBER.
KRISTY THOMAS IS THE PRESIDENT. THE CLUB WAS HER IDEA, AND SHE KEEPS EVERYTHING RUNNING PROFESSIONALLY.
WE HAVE TWO ASSOCIATE MEMBERS, ACTUALLY -- THE OTHER ONE IS SHANNON KILBOURNE. LOGAN AND SHANNON DON'T COME TO MEETINGS, BUT THEY TAKE JOBS WHEN WE NEED THE EXTRA HELP.

WELL, WE'VE NEVER SAT FOR A DEAF CHILD BEFORE, BUT THAT'S OKAY WITH US IF IT'S OKAY WITH YOU.

TRAINING? THAT MAKES SENSE.

LET ME TALK TO THE OTHER BABY-SITTERS AND I'LL CALL YOU BACK.
WHAT'S YOUR NUMBER?
OKAY... THANKS. BYE.

CLACK
THAT WAS A NEW CLIENT, MRS. BRADDOCK.

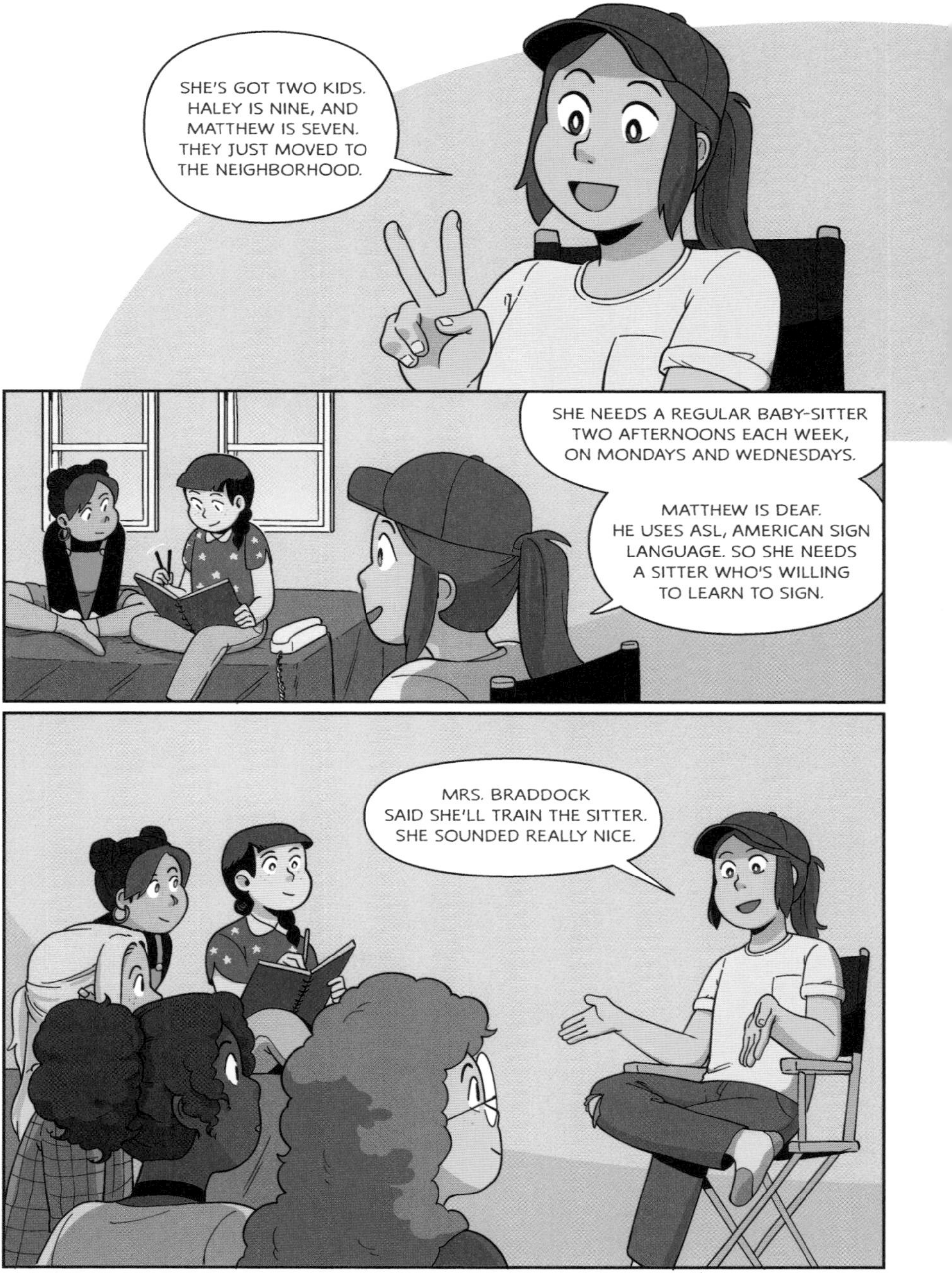

SHE'S GOT TWO KIDS. HALEY IS NINE, AND MATTHEW IS SEVEN. THEY JUST MOVED TO THE NEIGHBORHOOD.

SHE NEEDS A REGULAR BABY-SITTER TWO AFTERNOONS EACH WEEK, ON MONDAYS AND WEDNESDAYS.

MATTHEW IS DEAF. HE USES ASL, AMERICAN SIGN LANGUAGE. SO SHE NEEDS A SITTER WHO'S WILLING TO LEARN TO SIGN.

MRS. BRADDOCK SAID SHE'LL TRAIN THE SITTER. SHE SOUNDED REALLY NICE.

DAWN AND MARY ANNE DIDN'T WANT REGULAR AFTERNOON JOBS. THEY WANTED THEIR SCHEDULES TO BE MORE FREE.

CLAUDIA COULDN'T TAKE THE JOB BECAUSE SHE HAD AN ART CLASS ON WEDNESDAYS.

KRISTY LIVED TOO FAR AWAY TO BE CONVENIENT FOR THE JOB.

MAL WAS INTERESTED, BUT SHE OFTEN HAD TO WATCH HER BROTHERS AND SISTERS ON MONDAYS, WHEN HER MOM VOLUNTEERED.

SO KRISTY CALLED MRS. BRADDOCK BACK AND LET HER KNOW THAT I'D BE TAKING THE JOB!

I WAS EXCITED TO MEET A NEW FAMILY AND LEARN SIGN LANGUAGE.

HEY, JESSI!

HOW DID THE TRYOUTS GO?
OH, FINE!

BUT I WON'T KNOW ANYTHING UNTIL MY NEXT CLASS.

WELL, GOOD LUCK!

THANKS.

CHAPTER 3
THERE WERE ELEVEN OTHER GIRLS IN MY CLASS. I WAS THE YOUNGEST AND THE NEWEST.
AND ONE AND TWO
AND THREE AND FOUR
AND PLIÉ...
PLIÉ.
AND ONE
AND TWO
AND THREE...
HILARY AND KATIE BETH HAD BEEN THE YOUNGEST UNTIL I CAME ALONG. I COULD TELL THEY WERE UPSET.

THEY DID NOT LIKE ME.
ON YOUR TOES.
UP, UP, UP!

PAY ATTENTION, MADEMOISELLE RAMSEY!

WE FINISHED OUR BARRE WORK AND STARTED ON SOME FLOOR EXERCISES. TOUR JETÉS AND STUFF LIKE THAT.

MADAME BEGAN TO TEACH US A COMPLICATED ROUTINE THAT INVOLVED US DANCING WITH OUR HANDS CROSSED AND JOINED.

HILARY AND KATIE BETH WOULDN'T STOP GIVING ME DIRTY LOOKS.

OKAY, MES PETITES.
GATHER AROUND, PLEASE.
CLAP!

I AM GOING TO ANNOUNCE THOSE OF YOU WHO HAVE EARNED PARTS IN *COPPÉLIA*.

MARY BRAMSTEDT AND LISA JONES WILL BE TWO OF THE TOWNSPEOPLE.

CARRIE STEINFELD WILL PARTICIPATE IN THE DANCE OF THE HOURS.

HILARY, ALTHOUGH THE PORCELAIN DOLL IS USUALLY PLAYED BY A MALE DANCER, YOU HAVE BEEN GIVEN THAT PART.

KATIE BETH, YOU WILL PLAY COPPÉLIA.

AND, FINALLY, I AM VERY PLEASED TO ANNOUNCE THAT THE PART OF SWANILDA HAS BEEN AWARDED TO ONE OF THE STUDENTS IN THIS CLASS.

SWANILDA WILL BE PLAYED BY MADEMOISELLE JESSICA.

I ADMIT THAT JESSICA IS A BIT YOUNG FOR THE ROLE, BUT I THINK SHE CAN HANDLE IT. JESSICA, YOUR AUDITION WAS WONDERFUL.
THAT IS ALL. SATURDAY REHEARSALS WILL BEGIN THIS WEEKEND FOR THOSE IN THE PERFORMANCE.

CLASS IS DISMISSED.

I BEGAN TO IMAGINE MYSELF ONSTAGE IN SWANILDA'S LOVELY COSTUME. I SAW MYSELF PIROUETTING AND TOUR JETÉING.

CONGRATULATIONS, JESSI.

THANKS.

CONGRATULATIONS, **JESSI.**

HEHEHEHE
CONGRATULATIONS TO YOU, TOO.

THE PORCELAIN DOLL. THAT'S A GREAT PART. AND COPPÉLIA, KATIE BETH. THAT'S TERRIFIC.
OH, COME OFF IT. COPPÉLIA BARELY DOES ANYTHING.

SHE JUST SITS THERE. SHE'S A **DOLL,** FOR HEAVEN'S SAKE.

THEY COULD PUT A DUMMY ONSTAGE, AND IT WOULD BE THE SAME THING.
NO, IT WOULDN'T.

TCH!

TEACHER'S PET.

SHE JUST GOT THE PART BECAUSE SHE'S MADAME'S FAVORITE.
AND SHE'S THE FAVORITE BECAUSE SHE'S THE NEWEST AND YOUNGEST.

YEAH, JUST WAIT UNTIL ANOTHER GIRL JOINS THE CLASS.
THEN SHE'LL SEE.
CLICK

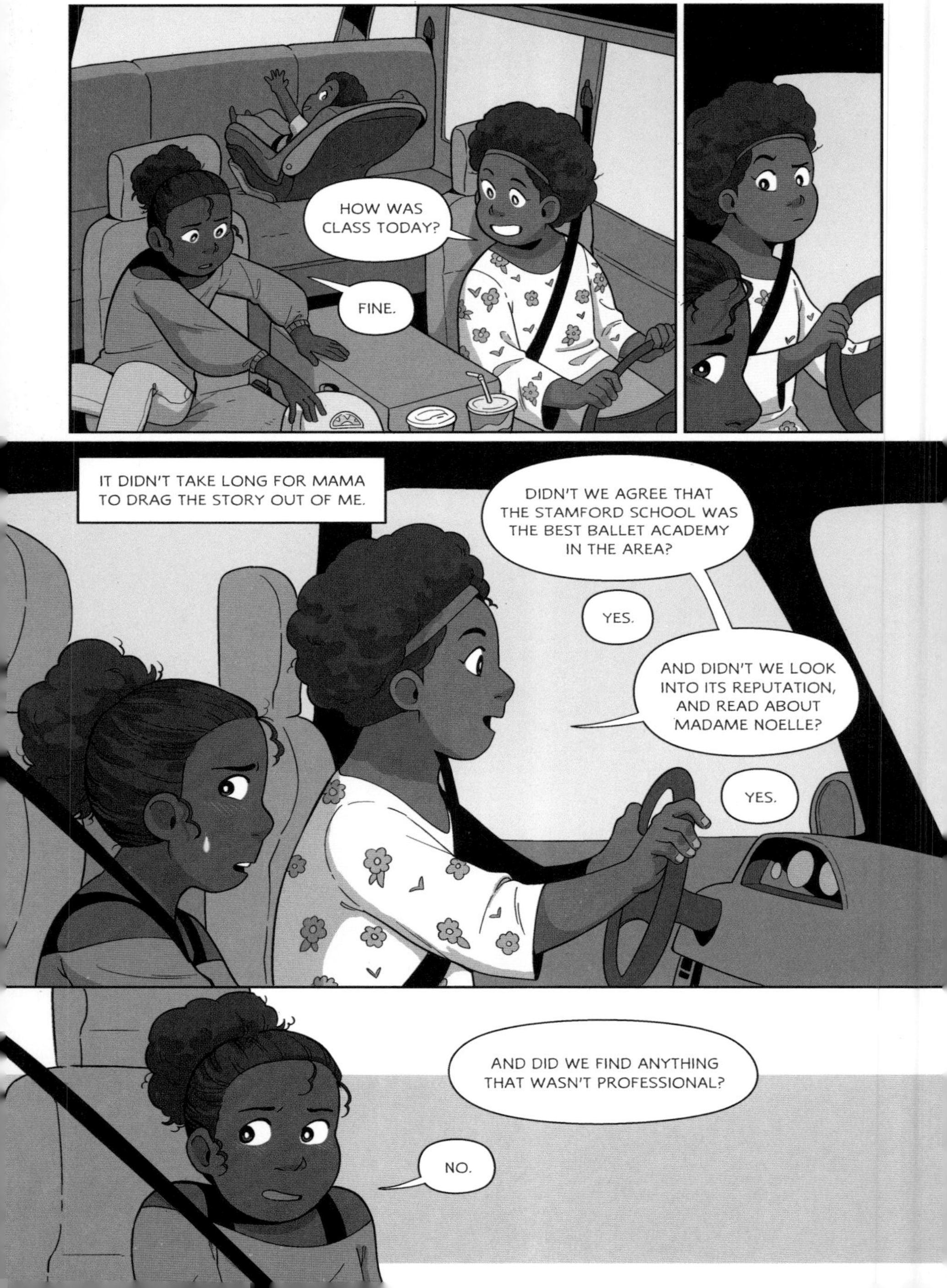

HOW WAS CLASS TODAY?

FINE.

IT DIDN'T TAKE LONG FOR MAMA TO DRAG THE STORY OUT OF ME.

DIDN'T WE AGREE THAT THE STAMFORD SCHOOL WAS THE BEST BALLET ACADEMY IN THE AREA?

YES.

AND DIDN'T WE LOOK INTO ITS REPUTATION, AND READ ABOUT MADAME NOELLE?

YES.

AND DID WE FIND ANYTHING THAT WASN'T PROFESSIONAL?
NO.

DO YOU REALLY THINK MADAME NOELLE WOULD RISK THE WHOLE SHOW AND CAST THE STARRING ROLE WITH A DANCER WHO WASN'T THE BEST FOR THE PART, JUST TO PLAY FAVORITES?
NOPE.
I DON'T THINK SO, EITHER.
WINK
THANKS, MAMA.

CHAPTER 4

DING-DONG

HI. ARE YOU JESSICA?
YUP, BUT CALL ME JESSI. YOU MUST BE HALEY.

YUP.
COME ON IN.

HI, JESSICA --
JESSI, MOMMY. CALL HER JESSI.

MATT HASN'T COME HOME FROM SCHOOL YET, BUT HE'LL BE HERE ANY MINUTE.

AS YOU KNOW, I'M NOT GOING OUT THIS AFTERNOON. I MEAN, YOU'RE NOT HERE FOR OFFICIAL BABY-SITTING. I JUST WANT YOU TO MEET MATT AND HALEY, AND I WANT TO INTRODUCE YOU TO SIGN LANGUAGE.

LET'S START. I LOVE LANGUAGES.
TERRIFIC.

CAN I BE THE TEACHER, MOMMY?
YOU BETTER BE THE ASSISTANT TEACHER, HONEY.
WHY DON'T YOU START BY FINDING THE AMERICAN SIGN LANGUAGE DICTIONARY?
DOES HALEY KNOW SIGN LANGUAGE, TOO?
WE ALL DO.
IT'S THE ONLY WAY TO COMMUNICATE WITH MATT, AND WE DON'T WANT HIM LEFT OUT OF ANYTHING.
BEFORE I BEGIN SHOWING YOU ACTUAL SIGNS, I SHOULD TELL YOU A LITTLE ABOUT TEACHING THE DEAF.
PAT PAT

ONE THING YOU OUGHT TO KNOW IS THAT NOT EVERYONE AGREES THAT THE DEAF SHOULD COMMUNICATE WITH SIGN LANGUAGE.
SOME PEOPLE THINK THEY SHOULD BE TAUGHT TO SPEAK AND TO READ LIPS.
HOWEVER, IN LOTS OF CASES, SPEAKING IS OUT OF THE QUESTION.
MATT, FOR INSTANCE, IS WHAT WE CALL PROFOUNDLY DEAF. THAT MEANS HE HAS ALMOST TOTAL HEARING LOSS. HE WAS BORN THAT WAY.
WE'RE NOT SURE HE'S EVER HEARD A SOUND IN HIS LIFE. HE DOESN'T EVEN WEAR HEARING AIDS. THEY WOULDN'T DO HIM ANY GOOD.
AND SINCE MATT CAN'T HEAR SOUNDS, HE CAN'T HEAR SPOKEN WORDS, OF COURSE, AND HE CAN'T IMITATE THEM, EITHER.
WHILE SOME PROFOUNDLY DEAF PEOPLE CAN SPEAK, IN MATT'S CASE THERE'S ALMOST NO CHANCE OF SPEECH. NOTHING THAT MOST PEOPLE COULD UNDERSTAND, ANYWAY.
AND LIPREADING IS HARD. I EXPERIMENTED IN FRONT OF THE MIRROR LAST NIGHT.

HOW COME SOME PEOPLE WANT DEAF KIDS TO SPEAK AND READ LIPS?
BECAUSE IF THEY COULD, THEY'D BE ABLE TO COMMUNICATE WITH SO MANY MORE HEARING PEOPLE.
IN HIS DAILY LIFE, MATT CAN COMMUNICATE ONLY WITH US AND WITH THE TEACHERS AND STUDENTS AT HIS SCHOOL.

NONE OF OUR FRIENDS KNOW SIGN LANGUAGE, AND ONLY A FEW OF OUR RELATIVES DO.
WHEN MATT GROWS OLDER, HE'LL MEET OTHER DEAF PEOPLE WHO USE SIGN LANGUAGE, AND MAYBE EVEN A FEW HEARING PEOPLE WHO CAN SIGN, BUT THE NUMBER OF PEOPLE HE'LL BE ABLE TO COMMUNICATE WITH WILL BE LIMITED.
IMAGINE GOING TO A MOVIE THEATER AND TRYING TO SIGN WHICH MOVIE YOU WANTED TO SEE BUT NO ONE KNOWING WHAT YOU MEANT.

WE'RE NOT SURE WE'VE MADE THE RIGHT CHOICE, BUT THAT'S THE CHOICE WE MADE. AT LEAST WE'VE BEEN ABLE TO COMMUNICATE WITH MATT FOR A LONG TIME NOW.
MOST KIDS TAKE YEARS TO LEARN LIPREADING AND FEEL FRUSTRATED CONSTANTLY, EVEN AT HOME. SOME FAMILIES DON'T BOTHER TO LEARN TO SIGN. THE DEAF CHILDREN IN THOSE FAMILIES MUST FEEL SO LOST.

HERE'S THE DICTIONARY.
PLOP
FWP
K
1
2
Key
OH, I GET IT! THIS LOOKS LIKE FUN.
IT IS SORT OF FUN. BUT THERE ARE SEVERAL THOUSAND SIGNS IN THERE.
SEVERAL **THOUSAND!**

DON'T WORRY. RIGHT NOW, I'M JUST GOING TO TEACH YOU A FEW OF THE SIGNS THAT MATT USES THE MOST.
WHEN YOU'RE AT HOME, YOU CAN USE THE DICTIONARY TO LOOK UP OTHER SIGNS OR THINGS YOU FORGET, OKAY?
OKAY.

CLICK

WELL, THERE YOU ARE! HOME FROM SCHOOL.

BELIEVE IT OR NOT, THE WAVE IS THE SIGN FOR "HELLO." IT'S ALSO THE SAME FOR "GOOD-BYE."
THAT'S EASY TO REMEMBER.

PLOP

THIS IS THE SIGN FOR MATT'S NAME.

HE'S HOLDING UP THE LETTER "M," FOR "MATT," WHILE DOING THE SIGN FOR "BASEBALL." MATT LOVES SPORTS.

NOW HE'S GOING TO SHOW THE SIGN FOR HALEY.

THAT WAS THE LETTER "H" SOARING LIKE HALLEY'S COMET.

IS THERE A SIGN FOR MY NAME?

THAT'S A GOOD QUESTION.

NOT YET -- WE'LL HAVE TO GIVE YOU ONE SOON.

THE WORD "YOU" IS EASY. JUST POINT TO THE PERSON YOU'RE TALKING TO.
MRS. BRADDOCK TAUGHT ME SO MUCH.
BATHROOM
APPLE
TO WANT
SORRY
DRINK

THANK YOU

OUTSIDE

PLAY

COME

SHE SHOWED ME SIGNS FOR FOODS, PARTS OF THE BODY, AND OTHER ESSENTIALS.

I THINK THAT'S ENOUGH FOR ONE DAY.

I'M GOING TO START DINNER. WHY DON'T YOU SPEND TIME WITH MATT AND HALEY SO YOU CAN GET TO KNOW THEM BETTER?
FWP FWP
CAN YOU ASK MATT WHAT HE WANTS TO PLAY?

HE WANTS TO READ.

HOW CAN I GET TO KNOW HIM IF HE READS?

HOW ABOUT GETTING TO KNOW **ME?**

THAT NIGHT, I WROTE DOWN A TON OF QUESTIONS FOR MRS. BRADDOCK.

HOW DO YOU SIGN A QUESTION? OR MAKE A WORD PLURAL? CAN YOU STRING SIGNS INTO SENTENCES? WHAT'S FINGER SPELLING?

EVEN THOUGH I KNEW I HAD A LOT TO LEARN, I DECIDED THAT I LIKED SIGN LANGUAGE.
CLICK

IT WAS VERY EXPRESSIVE...
ALMOST LIKE DANCING.

American
Sign
Language

Wednesday

Brat, brat, brat.

Okay. We all agree that Jenny is spoiled and a little bratty, but I've never minded her too much. At least, not until today. Today she was at her worst. Mostly, she just didn't want to do anything. She wasn't dressed for anything fun and she wouldn't change into play clothes. Finally, I took her outside and we ran into Jessi and the Braddocks! Then Jenny's brattiness just came pouring out. That kid needs a few lessons in manners. Really. Maybe we should start a class.

Mary Anne

CHAPTER 5

MARY ANNE'S AFTERNOON AT THE PREZZIOSOS' HOUSE BEGAN RIGHT AFTER SCHOOL ENDED.

FINISH UP YOUR PUDDING, JEN, AND THEN WE CAN PLAY SOME GAMES.

I EAT SLOWLY.

AND DON'T CALL ME JEN.

SORRY. I DIDN'T MEAN TO INSULT YOU.

ALL FINISHED.
GREAT. GO PUT THEM IN THE SINK.

LET'S PLAY A GAME. HOW ABOUT CANDY LAND? OR CHUTES AND LADDERS?
I DON'T WANNA.

THEN LET'S READ. WHERE'S *SQUIRREL NUTKIN*? THAT'S YOUR FAVORITE.
NO, IT ISN'T, AND I DON'T WANNA READ.

. . .
I KNOW!
FINGER PAINTING!
FINGER PAINTING?
REALLY?

YES...IF YOU CHANGE INTO PLAY CLOTHES.
NO. NO, NO, NO. THIS IS MY NEW DRESS, AND I'M WEARING IT.

OKAY, FINE.
IF THERE'S NOTHING YOU WANT TO DO, THEN YOU CAN JUST STAND HERE ALL AFTERNOON. I'M GOING TO READ A BOOK.

YOU MEAN YOU'RE NOT GOING TO PLAY WITH ME?
SIGH

WHAT DO YOU WANT TO PLAY?
I DON'T KNOW.
DOLLS?
NOPE.
HOUSE?
NOPE.
YOU WANT TO DRAW A NICE PICTURE FOR YOUR MOMMY?
NOPE.
SWING
THAT DOES IT.
WE'RE GOING...
OUTSIDE...
AND WE'RE GOING TO HAVE **FUN.**
TUG

CLICK

HI, JESSI!
HEY, MARY ANNE!

THIS IS MATT AND HALEY BRADDOCK.

AND THIS IS JENNY PREZZIOSO.

WHAT ARE YOU DOING?

MATT'S DEAF.
HE CAN'T HEAR US, BUT WE CAN TELL HIM THINGS WITH OUR HANDS. THEN HE CAN SEE WHAT WE'RE SAYING.

CAN'T YOU HEAR ME?
STUMBLE

CATCH

HE JUST SAID HI TO YOU.

YOU MEAN HE CAN'T TALK, EITHER?
HE CAN MAKE **SOUNDS.**
!

WIGGLE
WIGGLE

HAHAH
HAHAH

LET'S GO. HE'S WEIRD.
I DON'T WANT TO PLAY WITH HIM.

WELL, YOU'RE NOT THE FIRST ONE TO SAY SO!

WE BETTER LEAVE. I'M SORRY, JESSI.
I'LL CALL YOU TONIGHT SO WE CAN TALK, OKAY?
NOD

YOU KNOW WHAT?
HAVING A BROTHER LIKE MATT REALLY **STINKS.**
YOU **STINK,** MATT!
YOU **STINK!!!**

IT'S HORRIBLE! PEOPLE THINK MATT'S WEIRD, BUT **HE ISN'T.**
DEAF IS NOT WEIRD. EVERYBODY'S UNFAIR.
?

SLAM!

HALEY AND MATT HAD JUST MOVED TO A NEW NEIGHBORHOOD. HALEY WANTED TO FIT IN AND THOUGHT MATT MADE IT A LITTLE DIFFICULT.

I WAS BEGINNING TO UNDERSTAND THE SITUATION MORE...AND KNEW I HAD TO HELP HALEY SEE THINGS DIFFERENTLY.
WIGGLE

CHAPTER 6

I WAS MORE NERVOUS FOR MY NEXT BABY-SITTING JOB WITH HALEY AND MATT THAN I HAD BEEN AT THE MOST RECENT BALLET REHEARSAL.
DING-DONG
GETTING READY FOR *COPPÉLIA* WAS HARD WORK, BUT DANCING MOSTLY MADE ME SORE, NOT NERVOUS.
STRETCH
HI, JESSI. COME ON IN.
REMEMBER TO BE CAREFUL OUTDOORS. MATT CAN'T HEAR CAR HORNS.
AND HE CAN'T HEAR A SHOUTED WARNING.
AND INSIDE HE CAN'T HEAR THE DOORBELL OR TELEPHONE.
YUP.
RIGHT.
I'LL TAKE CARE OF THOSE THINGS.

DO YOU REMEMBER THE SIGN FOR "BATHROOM"?
YES!

FOR "EAT"?

I CAN DO FINGER SPELLING. I MEMORIZED THE ALPHABET LAST NIGHT.
THE WHOLE ALPHABET?
THE WHOLE THING. DON'T WORRY, MRS. BRADDOCK. MATT AND I WILL GET ALONG JUST FINE.

BESIDES, YOU'VE GOT ME, RIGHT?

I'LL SAY!

WELL...

MATT SHOULD BE HERE IN ABOUT TEN MINUTES. I TOLD HIM THIS MORNING THAT YOU WOULD BE HERE WHEN HE GOT HOME FROM SCHOOL AND THAT I'D BE BACK SOON.
HALEY CAN HELP YOU REMIND HIM IF HE SEEMS ANXIOUS, BUT I THINK HE'LL BE ALL RIGHT. HE REALLY LIKES YOU, JESSI.
THANKS.

ALL RIGHT. AFTER MATT PUTS AWAY HIS BAG, WE CAN GO FOR A WALK.

DASH

WHERE ARE WE GOING?
WE'RE GOING TO MY FRIEND MALLORY PIKE'S HOUSE. SHE HAS SEVEN BROTHERS AND SISTERS!

IS ONE OF THEM MY AGE?
YUP.

THE NINE-YEAR-OLD IS A GIRL. HER NAME IS VANESSA. SHE LIKES TO MAKE UP RHYMES.

IS THERE A SEVEN-YEAR-OLD PIKE?

YES. A GIRL.

THERE'S AN EIGHT-YEAR-OLD BOY, NICKY.
CAN YOU SIGN THAT FOR ME, HALEY?
DING-DONG
COME ON IN. EVERYONE'S PLAYING IN THE BACKYARD.
SUZI, BUDDY, AND MARNIE BARRETT ARE HERE, TOO.
THANKS, MAL.

HELLO!

THE INTRODUCTIONS BEGAN.

THE SIGNING BEGAN.

THE EXPLAINING BEGAN.

THE STARING BEGAN.

YOU KNOW, MAYBE MATT CAN'T HEAR OR TALK LIKE YOU, BUT HE KNOWS A **SECRET LANGUAGE.**
HE CAN SAY ANYTHING HE WANTS WITHOUT MAKING A SOUND.
REALLY?

THINK HOW USEFUL THAT WOULD BE IF, LIKE, MOM AND DAD PUNISHED YOU AND SAID, "NO TALKING FOR HALF AN HOUR." YOU COULD TALK AND THEY'D NEVER KNOW IT.
YEAH... AWESOME.
HOW DO YOU DO IT?

IT'S THIS.

WHOA!

SAY SOMETHING.
HE CAN'T HEAR YOU.

I'LL TELL HIM WHAT YOU SAID.

MATT SAYS HE THINKS THE PATRIOTS ARE GOING TO WIN THE SUPER BOWL THIS YEAR. HE SAYS --
NO WAY!

WHAT'S HE SAYING?
WHAT'S HE SAYING?

YOUR BROTHERS AND SISTERS ARE GREAT.

WHEN YOU GROW UP IN A FAMILY AS BIG AS MINE, YOU END UP BEING PRETTY ACCEPTING.
THANK GOODNESS.

HA HA HA HA HA HA

HEY, JESSI?

I HAD A GOOD
TIME. THANKS.

CHAPTER 7

CLAP
WE WANT PER-FEC-TION. NOTHING LESS.

MADEMOISELLE PARSONS, YOU MUST TURN YOUR HEAD FASTER AND START THE TURN A LITTLE LATER.

MADEMOISELLE BRAMSTEDT, HIGHER ON THE TOES. THIS IS A TOE-DANCING PRODUCTION.

MADEMOISELLE RAMSEY...

EXCELLENT WORK.

OKAY, CLASS. OUR TIME HAS ENDED. THIS WAS A GOOD REHEARSAL.
GO CHANGE. I WILL SEE YOU IN YOUR CLASSES NEXT WEEK.
TAP TAP
GOOD WORK.
YEAH, NICE JOB.

DADDY HAD SAID HE'D BE A LITTLE LATE PICKING ME UP. EVEN THOUGH IT WAS SATURDAY, HE WAS COMING FROM HIS OFFICE IN STAMFORD.

HE TOLD ME THAT HE'D PICK ME UP AT 4:30, AFTER SOME IMPORTANT MEETING.

THIS IS MY SISTER, ADELE.
HI, ADELE.

NUDGE

I'M WAITING FOR MY FATHER. HE WON'T BE HERE FOR FIFTEEN MORE MINUTES.

WE'RE WAITING FOR OUR MOM. SHE'S TALKING TO MADAME NOELLE. SHE'S UPSET BECAUSE I NEED NEW TOE SHOES SO OFTEN.
TAP TAP TAP

MY PARENTS DON'T LIKE IT, EITHER. BUT THERE'S REALLY NOTHING YOU CAN DO ABOUT IT.

FWP

THAT'S WHAT I TRIED TO TELL MOM, BUT --
TAP TAP TAP

HEY, KATIE BETH, ADELE CAN USE THE BATHROOM DOWN THE HALL.
NO ONE WOULD MIND.

BOUNCE

SHE HAD TO GO TO THE BATHROOM.
YOU MEAN YOU UNDERSTOOD HER?
YES. DIDN'T YOU?

NO.
I DON'T KNOW SIGN LANGUAGE.

YOU DON'T? BUT HOW DO YOU LIVE WITH ADELE?
OH, I DON'T LIVE WITH HER. NOT REALLY. SHE GOES TO A SPECIAL SCHOOL FOR THE DEAF. IT'S IN MASSACHUSETTS.

SHE LIVES THERE MOST OF THE TIME. SHE ONLY COMES HOME FOR HOLIDAYS, PART OF THE SUMMER, AND A FEW WEEKENDS.
BUT WHEN SHE'S HOME, HOW DO YOU TALK WITH HER?

WELL, I DON'T EXACTLY. I MEAN, MY PARENTS AND I DON'T.
SOMETIMES IF WE SHOUT REALLY LOUDLY, SHE CAN HEAR US A LITTLE. AND SHE CAN READ LIPS, SORT OF.

DOES SHE TALK?
NOPE.
SHE COULD, BUT SHE WON'T. SHE IS SO STUBBORN.

YOU KNOW, SIGN LANGUAGE IS FUN. AND IN A WAY, IT'S LIKE DANCING.

WHAT DO YOU MEAN?
WELL, IT'S A WAY OF EXPRESSING YOURSELF USING YOUR BODY.
I COULD SHOW YOU SOME SIGNS.
I DON'T KNOW...

OH, COME ON. IT'S FUN. LOOK! THIS IS THE SIGN FOR "DANCE."

OH, COOL!

TUG

"ARE YOU A DANCER?"

"YES."

WH-WHAT ARE YOU SAYING?
I TOLD HER. THEN I SHOWED HER THE SIGNS FOR A FEW MORE WORDS.
BY THE TIME ADELE AND KATIE BETH'S MOM SHOWED UP, IT WAS ALMOST 4:30, SO I WALKED OUTSIDE WITH THEM AND WAITED FOR DADDY'S CAR.
GOOD-BYE! AND THANKS!
SEE YOU ON TUESDAY!
BYE!

CHAPTER 8
I WAS BABY-SITTING REGULARLY AT THE BRADDOCKS' NOW. I LOVED IT, BUT MY SCHEDULE WAS TOUGH.
YAAAWWWNNNN
ON TUESDAY AND FRIDAY, I WENT TO MY DANCE CLASS AND SOMETIMES STAYED LATER THAN USUAL.
REHEARSALS WERE HELD ON THE WEEKENDS, AND OFTEN ON THURSDAY AS WELL, WHICH HAD BEEN MY ONLY FREE AFTERNOON.
EVERY MONDAY AND WEDNESDAY AFTERNOON, I WENT DIRECTLY FROM SCHOOL TO MATT AND HALEY'S HOUSE.
THE SECRET LANGUAGE WAS SPREADING FAST. REMEMBERING SIGNS WAS A GAME, AND THE KIDS LEARNED QUICKLY.

WHERE'S VANESSA?
SHE HAD TO GO TO THE DENTIST.
OH.
WHAM

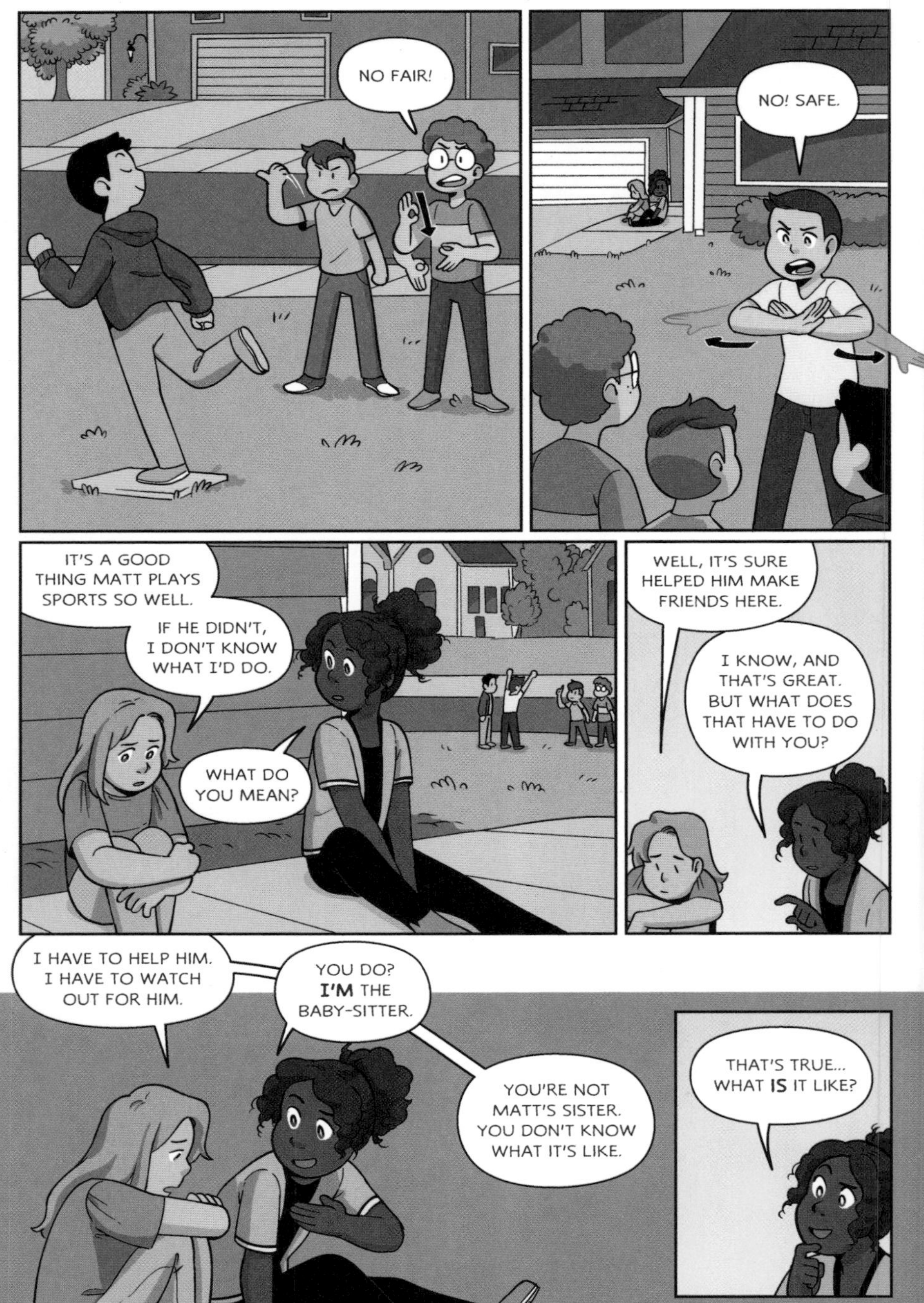

NO FAIR!
NO! SAFE.
IT'S A GOOD THING MATT PLAYS SPORTS SO WELL.
IF HE DIDN'T, I DON'T KNOW WHAT I'D DO.
WHAT DO YOU MEAN?
WELL, IT'S SURE HELPED HIM MAKE FRIENDS HERE.
I KNOW, AND THAT'S GREAT. BUT WHAT DOES THAT HAVE TO DO WITH YOU?
I HAVE TO HELP HIM. I HAVE TO WATCH OUT FOR HIM.
YOU DO? **I'M** THE BABY-SITTER.
YOU'RE NOT MATT'S SISTER. YOU DON'T KNOW WHAT IT'S LIKE.
THAT'S TRUE... WHAT **IS** IT LIKE?

YOU HAVE TO STAND UP FOR HIM WHEN KIDS TEASE HIM. BUT WHILE YOU'RE DOING IT, YOU WISH YOU DIDN'T HAVE TO.
IT MAKES ME HATE HIM SOMETIMES.
WELL, NOT HATE HIM. BUT... OH, WHAT'S THE WORD?
YOU RESENT MATT?
YEAH.
DON'T FEEL BAD ABOUT THAT. I RESENT MY BROTHER AND SISTER SOMETIMES, TOO.
LIKE WHEN MAMA ASKS ME TO GIVE SQUIRT A BATH AND I'D RATHER PRACTICE MY BALLET.
BUT YOUR BROTHER AND SISTER AREN'T DEAF.
WHY SHOULD YOU HAVE TO BE A PERFECT PERSON JUST BECAUSE YOUR BROTHER IS DEAF?
HE...
SQUEEEEEZE

HE MAKES IT HARD FOR ME TO MAKE MY OWN FRIENDS.
I REALLY LOVE HIM. AND I'M PROUD OF HIM. HE'S SMART, HE WORKS HARD, AND EVEN THOUGH HE'S DIFFERENT, HE GETS THINGS DONE HIS OWN WAY. BUT...
BUT IT'S STILL DIFFICULT FOR YOU TO LIVE YOUR OWN LIFE. I CAN UNDERSTAND THAT. I REALLY CAN.
SOMETIMES I THINK, BOY, WOULDN'T IT BE GREAT TO BE AN ONLY CHILD.
NO ONE WOULD EVER INTERRUPT ME WHILE I WAS PRACTICING OR TRYING TO DO MY HOMEWORK, AND NO ONE WOULD EVER SNOOP IN MY ROOM OR TAKE MY THINGS WITHOUT ASKING.
BUT THEN I THINK, IF I DIDN'T HAVE MY SISTER, BECCA, WHO COULD I GIGGLE WITH LATE AT NIGHT? AND WHO COULD I COMPLAIN TO?
I GREW UP LIVING CLOSE TO MY COUSINS, AND ONE OF THEM, KEISHA, WAS MY BEST FRIEND. MAKING FRIENDS IN STONEYBROOK HAS BEEN HARD.
EVERYONE ALREADY HAD THEIR CLIQUES HERE, AND I WAS THE NEW KID. BECCA IS THE ONLY PERSON I KNOW WHO SHARES THAT EXACT EXPERIENCE.

THAT MAKES SENSE. SOMETIMES...I'LL BE TOTALLY MAD AT MATT FOR EMBARRASSING ME, AND THEN I'LL REMEMBER THIS...
AND CAN'T FEEL MAD AT HIM AT ALL.
MATT MADE THIS IN ART CLASS AND GAVE IT TO ME FOR CHRISTMAS LAST YEAR. I ALWAYS WEAR IT.
SOMETIMES I DON'T KNOW WHAT I'D DO WITHOUT HIM. EVEN THOUGH I GET UPSET, I JUST WANT TO, YOU KNOW, PROTECT HIM AND STUFF.
AND THAT'S A VERY ADMIRABLE THING FOR YOU TO DO. NOT JUST AS A SISTER...
BUT AS A PERSON.

YOU KNOW, MAYBE HE CAN'T TALK WELL OR HEAR, BUT THINK OF WHAT HE CAN DO.
ALMOST ANYTHING.

HE CAN EVEN WATCH TV WITH SUBTITLES. SO REALLY THE ONLY THING MATT CAN'T EASILY DO IS GO TO A CONCERT OR A PLAY OR SOMETHING.
WHAM

MATT'S NEVER BEEN IN A THEATER? HE'S NEVER BEEN TO ANY KIND OF PERFORMANCE?
WELL, SOMETIMES HIS SCHOOL PUTS ON PLAYS IN SIGN LANGUAGE.

BUT IMAGINE. NEVER BEEN TO A BALLET OR A MUSICAL...
WELL, HE COULDN'T HEAR THE MUSIC.
I KNOW.

I THOUGHT ABOUT HOW MUCH MORE THERE WAS TO BALLET THAN THE MUSIC.
TAP
TAP
TAP
AND ONE AND TWO AND THREE AND FOUR...
CLAP
AND ONE AND TWO AND THREE AND FOUR...
CLAP
THERE WAS PLENTY TO SEE.
TAP
TAP
TAP
TAP
TAK

THERE WAS A LOT
TO FEEL, TOO.
LIKE THE STRONG HUMS
OF THE PIANO.
AND THE VIBRATIONS FROM
PEOPLE DANCING IN STEP.
PLUS, IT WAS JUST
PLAIN EXCITING TO BE
IN A THEATER.
ALL OF THIS
GAVE ME AN IDEA.

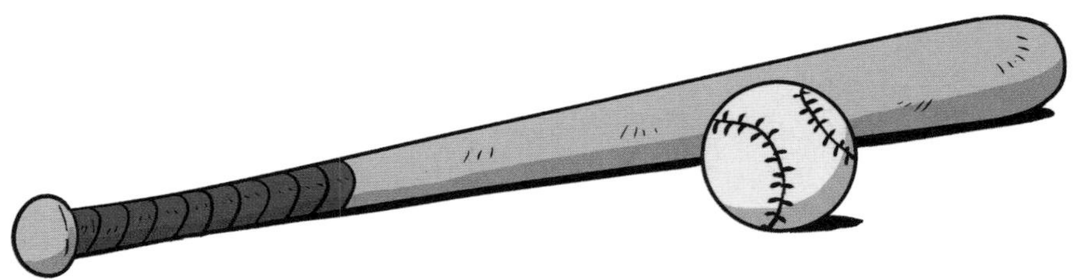

CHAPTER 9

YOU DIDN'T MISS MUCH. I WAS JUST SAYING HOW MY BROTHER CALLED FROM CALIFORNIA LAST NIGHT.
HE'S STILL REALLY HAPPY OUT THERE.
YOU THINK HE'LL STAY?
I'M PRETTY SURE HE WILL.
WHEN THE SIX MONTHS ARE UP, THE LAWYERS AND EVERYONE HAVE TO GET TOGETHER AGAIN TO DISCUSS THE TRIAL PERIOD...
BUT I KNOW HE'LL STAY.

OKAY. CLUB BUSINESS. ANYTHING URGENT?
CLAP

THE TREASURY'S LOW.
HOW'D THAT HAPPEN?
MOSTLY PAYING CHARLIE TO DRIVE YOU TO AND FROM MEETINGS.
WELL, DUES DAY IS COMING UP.

ONE DAY OF DUES ISN'T GOING TO HELP MUCH.
WELL, COULD ALL OF YOU KICK IN DOUBLE NEXT TIME...
JUST THIS ONCE?
SURE.
OKAY.

RING
RING

ANY OTHER BUSINESS?

I HAVE SOMETHING!

WHAT'S UP, JESSI?

I TOLD THEM THAT MATT AND HALEY WERE MAKING FRIENDS, AND FILLED THEM IN ON THE CONVERSATION I'D HAD WITH HALEY ABOUT WHAT IT WAS LIKE TO BE MATT'S BIG SISTER.
IS ANYONE INTERESTED IN LEARNING MORE ABOUT SIGNING?
YEAH!
LET'S DO IT!
REALLY?
SURE. ALL THE KIDS AROUND HERE ARE LEARNING TO SIGN. WE BETTER LEARN HOW, TOO.
RIGHT. BESIDES, US BABY-SITTERS HAVE TO BE PREPARED FOR ANYTHING.
RING RING

HEY, ONE OF YOU GUYS WANT TO GET THE PHONE?

RING RING RING

HELLO, BABY-SITTERS CLUB!

OH, YES. HI, MRS. BRADDOCK...
TELL HER WHAT?
OH, OKAY. SURE...BYE.

MRS. BRADDOCK SAID TO GIVE YOU A MESSAGE: EVERYTHING IS ARRANGED.
IT IS?!

OH, THAT'S GREAT. REALLY GREAT!

ARE YOU GOING TO LET US IN ON WHAT'S GOING ON?
YEAH. WHAT'S ARRANGED?

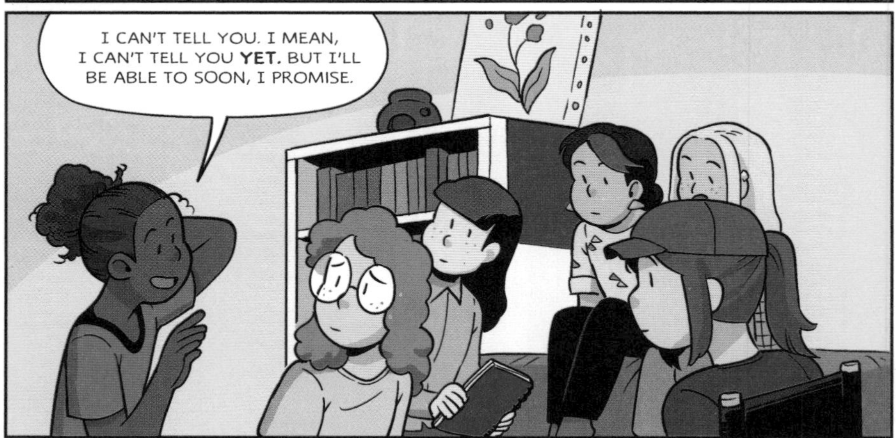
I CAN'T TELL YOU. I MEAN, I CAN'T TELL YOU **YET.** BUT I'LL BE ABLE TO SOON, I PROMISE.

HOW COME YOU CAN'T TELL US NOW?
I JUST CAN'T, THAT'S ALL.

BUT I DO WANT TO ASK YOU SOMETHING...

I WAS WONDERING IF YOU'D LIKE TO COME SEE *COPPÉLIA.* EVERYONE IN THE CAST GETS TEN FREE TICKETS TO OPENING NIGHT, SO I'M INVITING MAMA, DADDY, BECCA, GRANDMA, GRANDPA...AND YOU GUYS.

OPENING NIGHT!
THE BALLET!
GOING TO STAMFORD!

I TOOK THEIR REACTION AS A YES.

CHAPTER 10

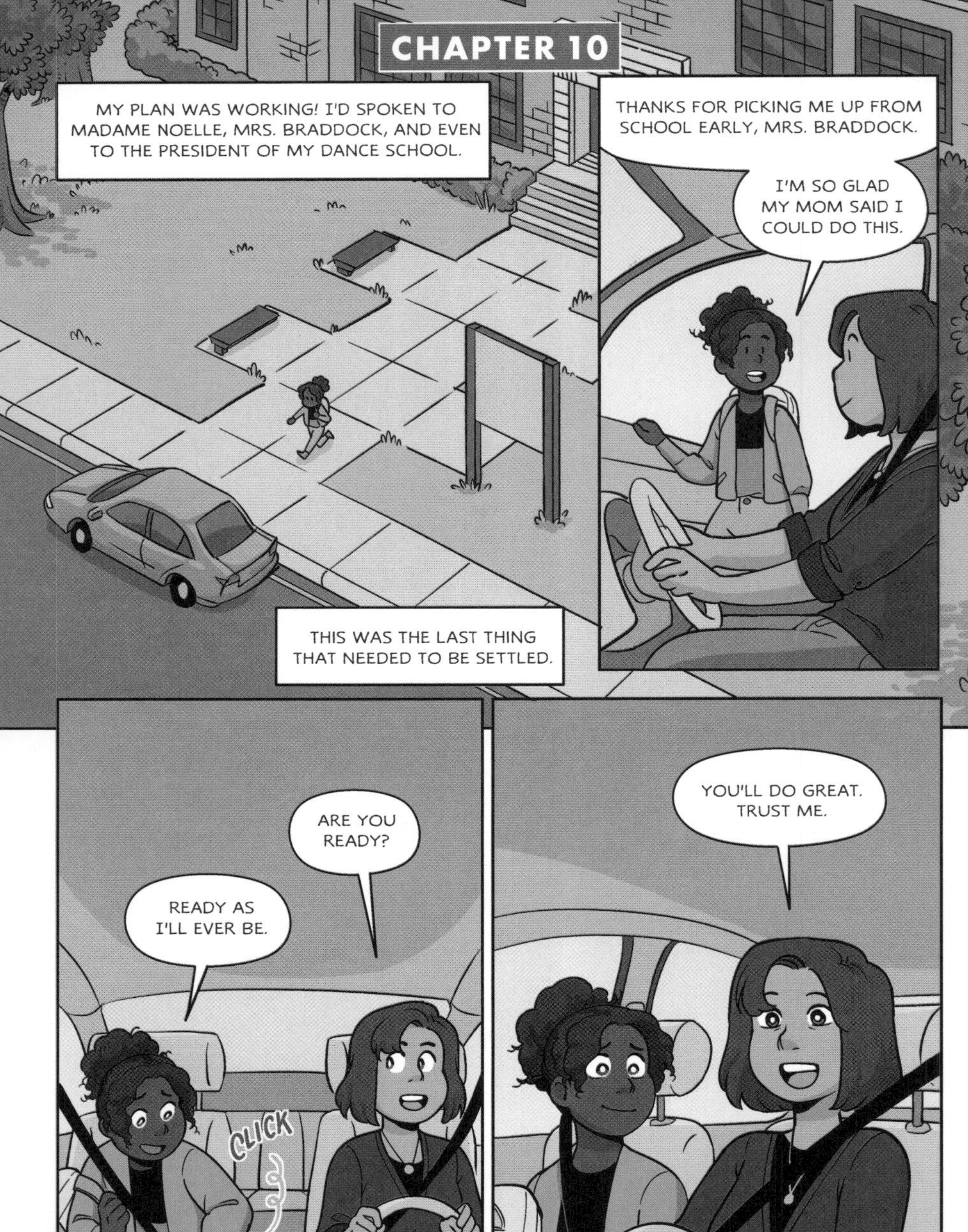

MY PLAN WAS WORKING! I'D SPOKEN TO MADAME NOELLE, MRS. BRADDOCK, AND EVEN TO THE PRESIDENT OF MY DANCE SCHOOL.
THIS WAS THE LAST THING THAT NEEDED TO BE SETTLED.
THANKS FOR PICKING ME UP FROM SCHOOL EARLY, MRS. BRADDOCK.
I'M SO GLAD MY MOM SAID I COULD DO THIS.
ARE YOU READY?
READY AS I'LL EVER BE.
CLICK
YOU'LL DO GREAT. TRUST ME.

SCHOOL FOR THE DEAF.

MATT WAS TWO WHEN HE ENTERED, AND THE TEACHERS BEGAN LESSONS IN SIGNING RIGHT AWAY.

THE YOUNGER CLASSES ARE ON THIS FLOOR. MATT'S IS AT THE VERY END OF THE CORRIDOR.

THE CHILDREN IN HIS CLASS ARE ALL SEVEN YEARS OLD. SOME ARE DEAF, AND SOME ARE HARD OF HEARING.
SINCE SOME OF THE CHILDREN CAN HEAR, AND SOME ARE LEARNING SPEECH AND LIPREADING, MAKE SURE YOU SPEAK CLEARLY WHILE LOOKING AT THE STUDENTS.

MS. FRANK OR I WILL INTERPRET INTO ASL FOR YOU. SINCE EACH LANGUAGE HAS ITS OWN GRAMMAR AND STRUCTURE, IT'S HARD TO DO BOTH PRECISELY AT THE SAME TIME.
RIGHT.

WELL...ARE YOU READY, JESSI?
I HOPE SO.
DON'T BE TOO NERVOUS. THEY LOVE VISITORS. AND MATT'S TEACHER AND I WILL HELP YOU IF YOU NEED IT.
OKAY.
HELLO, MRS. BRADDOCK.
YOU MUST BE JESSI.

I'M MS. FRANK, MATT'S TEACHER. THANK YOU SO MUCH FOR COMING.
THE CHILDREN ARE THRILLED, EVEN THOUGH THEY DON'T KNOW WHY YOU'RE HERE. ALL I'VE SAID IS THAT YOU HAVE A SURPRISE FOR THEM.
BEFORE I INTRODUCE YOU, THOUGH, I JUST WANT TO SAY THAT YOUR IDEA IS MARVELOUS.
IT'LL BE A GREAT EXPERIENCE FOR THE CHILDREN.
WHY DON'T YOU SIT ON THE FLOOR WITH THE KIDS?
YOU'LL ALL FEEL MORE AT EASE.

BOYS AND GIRLS,
THIS IS JESSI RAMSEY.

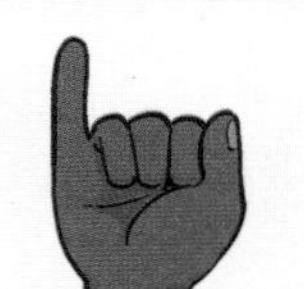

JESSI IS HERE BECAUSE SHE KNOWS MATT AND HAS A VERY SPECIAL SURPRISE FOR YOU.

JESSI?
THANKS.

I AM A DANCER. I LIKE DANCING BECAUSE I CAN TELL A STORY WITH MY BODY.
I DON'T NEED TO TALK.

A BALLET TELLS A STORY WITHOUT ANY WORDS -- JUST DANCE AND MUSIC.
I KNOW SOME OF YOU CAN'T HEAR MUSIC, BUT DID YOU KNOW THAT YOU CAN FEEL IT?
THEY'RE LEARNING ABOUT THAT NOW. WE'VE BEEN EXPERIMENTING WITH VIBRATION, RHYTHM, DRUMBEATS, AND THE PIANO.
OH, GOOD.
MY DANCE SCHOOL IS GOING TO PERFORM A BALLET CALLED *COPPÉLIA.* IT'S ABOUT A TOYMAKER AND A SPECIAL DOLL THAT HE CREATES. EVERYONE WILL WEAR COSTUMES, AND THE STAGE WILL LOOK LIKE A VILLAGE.
I WOULD VERY MUCH LIKE FOR YOU TO COME SEE *COPPÉLIA.* I KNOW YOU MIGHT NOT BE ABLE TO HEAR THE MUSIC, BUT YOU CAN WATCH THE DANCERS TELL THEIR STORY.
DO YOU WANT TO COME?
YES!!!

THE STORY OF *COPPÉLIA* IS A LITTLE COMPLICATED, SO I'LL TELL IT TO YOU BEFORE YOU GO TO THE SHOW.

HE ASKS, "WHEN IS THE SHOW?"
NEXT FRIDAY. EIGHT DAYS FROM NOW.

WHAT SHOULD WE WEAR?
WHATEVER YOU WANT, BUT IT MIGHT BE FUN TO GET DRESSED UP.

RRRIIIIIIIINNGGG

OKAY, CLASS, LET'S TELL JESSI THAT WE'LL SEE HER SOON!
SEE YOU SOON!
BYE!
MATT WANTED TO SHOW ME HIS DESK BEFORE WE LEFT.
OOOH!
HUG!

"YOU'RE MY BEST GROWN-UP FRIEND."
OH, MATT...

CHAPTER 11

OPENING NIGHT. I WAS NERVOUS, BUT NOT TOO MUCH. THIS PERFORMANCE WOULD BE DIFFERENT FROM ANY OTHER.

I COULDN'T WAIT TO SEE MATT'S CLASS IN THE AUDIENCE.

I'D KEPT THE SECRET FOR AS LONG AS I COULD. I FINALLY TOLD THE REST OF THE BSC THE NEWS TWO NIGHTS AGO.

YOU DID THAT FOR MATT?
YOU **ORGANIZED** ALL THAT?
YEAH! I DIDN'T WANT TO TELL YOU UNTIL EVERYTHING HAD COME TOGETHER.
I FELT GREAT.
THE PERFORMANCE WOULD START AT EIGHT O'CLOCK.
NOW IT WAS FIVE MINUTES TO EIGHT.

JESSI?

THE HOUSE IS PACKED. YOUR FRIENDS FROM THE SCHOOL FOR THE DEAF ARE SITTING IN THE CENTER FOURTH ROW.

OH, THANK YOU SO MUCH, MADAME. THAT'S WONDERFUL.

ARE YOU READY?
YES, I AM.

ALL RIGHT, THEN. GO AHEAD.

IT'LL BE OKAY.
LET'S GO.

GOOD EVENING!

TONIGHT'S PERFORMANCE IS A SPECIAL ONE. IN THE AUDIENCE ARE EIGHT STUDENTS FROM THE SCHOOL FOR THE DEAF HERE IN STAMFORD.

THIS IS CAROLYN BRADDOCK, THE MOTHER OF ONE OF THE STUDENTS...
AND THIS IS HALEY, HIS SISTER.

SO THAT THE STUDENTS CAN GET AS MUCH AS POSSIBLE OUT OF THE PERFORMANCE, HALEY IS GOING TO NARRATE THE STORY BEFORE EACH ACT, AND HER MOTHER WILL INTERPRET THE NARRATION INTO SIGN LANGUAGE.
THIS IS NOT USUALLY PART OF A PERFORMANCE OF *COPPÉLIA*, BUT WE HOPE YOU ENJOY IT ANYWAY.
THANK YOU.

UM...THE STORY BEGINS...

LOUDER!

CLAP
CLAP

SHAKE

YOU MIGHT THINK THAT I WAS AWARE OF THE FACT THAT MY FRIENDS AND FAMILY WERE IN THE AUDIENCE.

BUT I WASN'T. WHEN I'M ONSTAGE, I AM THE DANCE. I'M THE STEPS AND TURNS AND LEAPS.
I'M SWANILDA TELLING MY STORY. NOTHING LESS. FOR ME, THAT'S THE ONLY WAY TO HANDLE A PERFORMANCE.

ACT THREE IS THE LAST ACT OF THE BALLET. YOU WILL SEE THE DANCERS IN THE VILLAGE SQUARE AGAIN. FRANZ AND SWANILDA AREN'T MAD AT EACH OTHER ANYMORE, SO THEY DECIDE TO GET MARRIED, AND THEY GO TO THE BURGOMASTER FOR THEIR DOWRIES.

BUT JUST THEN, DR. COPPELIUS RUNS ANGRILY INTO THE SQUARE.
HE ACCUSES FRANZ AND SWANILDA OF WRECKING COPPÉLIA, WHICH WAS HIS LIFE'S WORK.

SINCE THEY DID DESTROY THE DOLL, SWANILDA GIVES THE MONEY FOR THE WEDDING TO DR. COPPELIUS.
HE IS PLEASED BY THAT, AND AFTER HE LEAVES, FRANZ AND SWANILDA GET MARRIED...AND I GUESS THEY LIVE HAPPILY EVER AFTER.

CLAP
CLAP
CLAP
CLAP

GREAT JOB.
YOU TOO.

CLAP
CLAP
CLAP
CLAP
CLAP

CHAPTER 12

TAP
TAP
CONGRATULATIONS!
HEY!
HI, HONEY!
HI, JESSI!
HELLO, DEAR.
FABULOUS SHOW!

JESS! I'M SO IMPRESSED!

HUG!

DO YOU KNOW HOW GLAD I AM THAT YOU'RE MY BEST FRIEND? I MEAN, NOT JUST BECAUSE OF THIS. YOU WERE ALREADY MY BEST FRIEND. BUT NOW YOU'RE A BALLET STAR, TOO. I CAN'T BELIEVE IT!
THANKS, MAL.

HI, JESSI.

I DON'T BELIEVE IT. I'M DREAMING, RIGHT?
THIS IS A DREAM.

I CAME WITH GRANDMA AND GRANDPA. YOUR PARENTS SENT ME A TICKET.

DID YOU LIKE THE SHOW?
IT WAS WONDERFUL. YOUR SHOWS ARE ALWAYS AMAZING.
OH, KEISHA.

LOOK AT US!

ARE YOU JESSI'S COUSIN?
OH! SORRY. I GUESS I SHOULD INTRODUCE YOU.

MAL, THIS IS MY COUSIN KEISHA, FROM OAKLEY.

THE ONE WITH THE SAME BIRTHDAY AS YOU?
NOD

AND, KEISHA, THIS IS MALLORY. SHE'S MY BEST --
UH...

I'VE HEARD A LOT ABOUT YOU, KEISHA. JESSI AND I HAVE TONS OF THINGS IN COMMON, BUT **NOT** THE SAME BIRTHDAY.
THAT'S REALLY SPECIAL. I WISH I HAD A COUSIN MY AGE WHO WAS MY BEST FRIEND.
I LIKE HER.

HEY! LOOK WHO'S HERE.

DURING THE PERFORMANCE, MATT CAME UP WITH A NAME SIGN FOR YOU.
REALLY?!

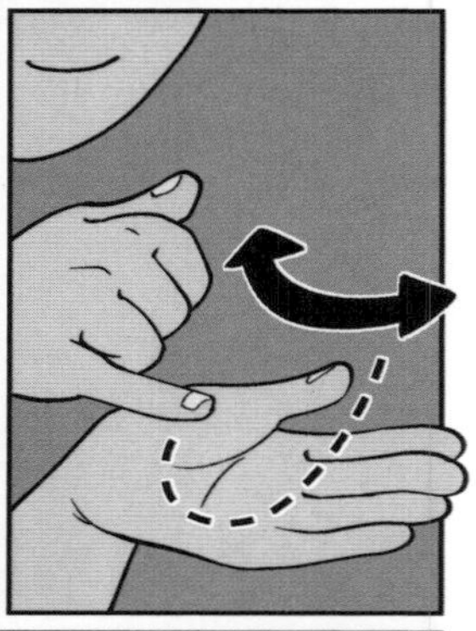

OH! LIKE A DANCING "J."

DID THE KIDS ENJOY THE SHOW?
IMMENSELY. THEY SAID THAT THEY COULD FEEL THE VIBRATIONS AND FOLLOW ALONG JUST FINE.

AND OUR NARRATION AND INTERPRETATION BEFORE EVERY ACT HELPED, TOO, RIGHT?
YES, OF COURSE.
HEHEHEHE

BUMP!

ADELE! WHAT A SURPRISE!

I DIDN'T KNOW YOU'D BE VISITING FROM MASSACHUSETTS. I'M REALLY GLAD YOU CAME.

NOD

SHE SAID SHE WANTED TO SEE US DANCE.

AND THAT SHE'D NEVER BEEN ASKED TO ATTEND A SHOW BEFORE.

I SEE...UM...
LISTEN, JESSI, I WANT TO...TELL YOU SOMETHING.
I BETTER GET MY COAT.
I'LL SEE YOU IN A FEW MINUTES.
WHAT IS IT?
YOU WERE... YOU WERE GOOD TONIGHT, JESSI. REALLY GOOD.
MADAME MADE THE RIGHT DECISION WHEN SHE PICKED YOU TO BE SWANILDA. I WAS JEALOUS BEFORE...
BUT I'VE GOT TO LEARN THAT NOT EVERYONE CAN HAVE THE LEAD.

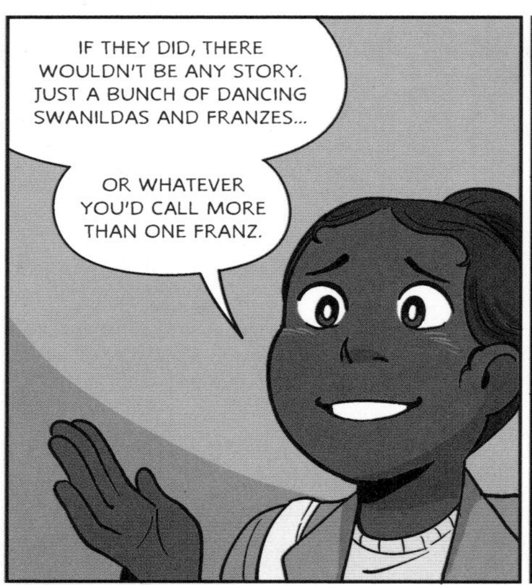
IF THEY DID, THERE WOULDN'T BE ANY STORY. JUST A BUNCH OF DANCING SWANILDAS AND FRANZES...
OR WHATEVER YOU'D CALL MORE THAN ONE FRANZ.

HAHAHAHAHAHA!

A-AND GUESS WHAT.
I'M LEARNING HOW TO SIGN. THERE'S A CLASS AT THE SCHOOL THAT MATT GOES TO. I FOUND OUT ABOUT IT ALL BY MYSELF.
ADELE IS MY ONLY SIBLING. SHE'S NOT AROUND MUCH, BUT WHEN SHE IS, IT'D BE NICE FOR US TO BE ABLE TO TALK LIKE SISTERS USUALLY DO.

THAT'S GREAT, KATIE BETH! IF YOU EVER NEED ANY HELP, LET ME KNOW.
THANKS.
OF COURSE.

KATIE BETH!
THAT'S MY MOM. WE BETTER GO.
OKAY.

JESSI, LET'S GET A MOVE ON.
EVERYONE IS READY TO LEAVE.

CHAPTER 13

ARE YOU ALL
READY TO ORDER?

THAT'S IT!
A BUTTERSCOTCH
SUNDAE!

I WOULD LIKE THE AMBROSIA,
AND HE WANTS THE BANANA
SPLIT SUNDAE.
A STRAWBERRY
MILKSHAKE FOR
ME, PLEASE.

YOUR ORDER
WILL BE COMING
RIGHT UP.
THANK YOU!

BOY, WHAT A TREAT! THIS HAS BEEN REALLY FUN.
I WASN'T SURE I'D LIKE BALLET, BUT I DID. I ESPECIALLY LIKED SEEING YOU, JESSI.
THANKS.

CLAUDIA, THAT IS **SO** GROSS.
SMUSH SMUSH

I WONDER IF THERE'S A SIGN FOR "GROSS."
THERE'S ONE FOR "GROTESQUE."

AND FOR "**DISGUSTING.**"

MUNCH
MUNCH
MUNC
SMUSH
SMUSH

MATT SAYS HE'S HAPPY.
HA HA HA
PAT
PAT

VERY HAPPY.

ANN M. MARTIN'S The Baby-sitters Club is one of the most popular series in the history of publishing — with more than 190 million books in print worldwide — and inspired a generation of young readers. Her novels include *Belle Teal, A Corner of the Universe* (a Newbery Honor book), *Here Today, A Dog's Life,* and *On Christmas Eve,* as well as the much-loved collaborations, *P.S. Longer Letter Later* and *Snail Mail No More,* with Paula Danziger, and *The Doll People* and *The Meanest Doll in the World,* written with Laura Godwin and illustrated by Brian Selznick. Ann lives in upstate New York.

CHAN CHAU is the creator of the *New York Times* bestselling graphic novel adaptation of *Kristy and the Snobs* by Ann M. Martin. They graduated from the Minneapolis College of Art and Design. Their work appears in the award-winning comics anthology *ELEMENTS: Fire*, and they have designed backgrounds for animated TV shows. Chan lives in Tacoma, Washington. Visit them online at chanchauart.com.

DON'T MISS THE OTHER BABY-SITTERS CLUB GRAPHIC NOVELS!